Tap Tap

Written by Jan Burchett
and Sara Vogler
Photographed by Will Amlot

Collins

a tin

tap tap

tip tap

tip tap

a pan

tin pan

tap tap

tap tap

tip pips in

tip tip

tip a tin

tip tip

/p/

14

❧ After reading ❧

Letters and Sounds: Phase 2

Word count: 26

Focus phonemes: /s/ /a/ /t/ /p/ /i/ /n/

Curriculum links: Expressive Arts: Exploring and Using Media and Materials

Early learning goals: Understanding: answer "how" and "why" questions about their experiences and in response to stories or events; Reading: children read and understand simple sentences, use phonic knowledge to decode regular words and read them aloud accurately, read some common irregular words

Developing fluency

- Your child may enjoy hearing you read the book.
- Encourage your child to read the book again, this time acting out the actions and sounds. You may wish to model reading the first few pages like this and ask your child to continue with the rest of the book.

Phonic practice

- Help your child to practise sounding out and blending CVC words that contain the /p/ sound.

t/a/p	tap
p/i/p/s	pips
t/i/p	tip

- Look at the "I spy sounds" pages (14–15). Say the sound together. How many items can your child spot with the /p/ sound in them? (e.g. *potatoes, pan, pepper, plum, pear, peach, plates, paper towel*)

Extending vocabulary

- Look at pages 4 and 5 together and talk about all of the words that could be used to describe a noise or sound. (*tip, tap*)
- Ask your child if they can think of any other words that describe a noise or sound. (e.g. *bang, pop, scream*)